Going Down on Her

Nacir Poorarianne

Edited by

Natalie André

D1715916

© 2020 Nacir Poorarianne

All rights reserved. No part of this e-book may be reproduced or retransmitted in any manner except in the form of a review, without written permission from the publisher.

This is a work of fiction. All characters, names, places and events are the product of the author's imagination or used fictitiously.

Author: Nacir Poorarianne

Editor: Natalie André

Cover design: Sigolene Sarkozy

Warning!

The following text contains explicit language and graphic sexual references.

Table of Contents

Beautiful Boss

Recently I visited an astonishing concert in Stuttgart, performed by one of my favorite German DJs called Schiller. He's a virtuoso music-composer and song-writer who according to Wikipedia, has sold more than seven million albums worldwide. I and my company were sitting in a huge arena, which belongs to Porsche Company. It's called Porsche Arena and is located in Stuttgart's outskirts, near to the venue where the so called folk festival, a combination of beer festival and travelling funfair is held.

As a half German--father side--and half foreign individual, that's to say as some-one who's not a pure German and to some extent an outsider, I dare say that I appreciate Germans for a number of things. Some of them being making good music, producing perfect cars, dressing fashionably and looking good, and last not least for their incredibly fascinating sense of harmony. It was not only the band itself, com-posed of several guitarists, singers, and drum kit players which were performing with amazing order and concord, but also a pleasant aroma and patterns of amazingly beautiful beams of lasers bestowed an unimaginable feeling on the air.

As I was amazed and absorbed in a fit of trance, suddenly the apparition of a woman dancing in front of me brought me back to my senses. She was dancing softly to the rhythmic melody of that great artist, shaking her beautiful, shapely body in ways I had never seen. I was fascinated by her steps and gestures, and looked up to see that beautiful face.

My heart missed a beat! I knew that woman, she looked older now, but still as beautiful…

$$\Omega \quad \Omega \quad \Omega$$

It'd been about ten years ago. I was 21 years old. I was a student of engineering in Düsseldorf University, and was almost at the end of my studies. However, I'd run out of money, and could not even pay my apartment's rent. In addition, although my father refused to support me, I still couldn't apply for the state's financial help for young students, called BAföG in Germany, because this aid belongs to people from poor families. It was an entangled legal situation on which I don't want to elaborate.

$$\Omega \quad \Omega \quad \Omega$$

Having come back from university after drinking a cup of coffee with my fellow student, Natalie, I call my father walking down Ettinger Street. After some small talk, I pose my urgent request in an imploring manner:

"Father I really need some money, I promise I'll repay it as soon as I can."

"I don't believe you. Have you forgotten? You owe me already much."

"What do I owe you?"

"I lent you €800 last December, do you remember?"

"What? Which €800? I think you mean those 400 bucks."

"Oh son! How long are you going to depend on me for money? You're like a beg-gar. Why do you ask me? Why don't you just go and accost people on the street? Maybe that way you can earn money faster than by pleading with me."

He hangs up. I take off my gloves and blow into my frosted hands. I then rub them together, hardly, more hardly, while I think no matter how cold I feel, I still feel warmer outside than inside, in my heart. My conversation with my father was a sheer frost. I try to think of other people and if they'd help me out of this predicament. I call Petra, my ex.

"Didn't I tell you that you should never call me again?"

"When did you say this? I don't remember."

She hangs up. It went really fast.

I feel helpless, I pace down Ettinger street towards the bus stop. I mull my conversation with Natalie. She is a good, kind woman. Few people are as good in this world. She cares about her friends and colleagues. She noticed that I have not been in a good mood for many days now. She invited me to coffee with a big smile this morning. It was the only moment I felt okay today. I tried several times to tell her about my problem and ask her for help, but I didn't dare do so. I feared she would shun me in case I would.

She told me I should remain hopeful about my life. That I should do new, exciting things, like going to a fitness studio, to a dance course, or learning to play a musical instrument. Or I should try to find a girlfriend. Maybe having someone new in my life could shore me up. She had no clue my main problem was money. She thought I had some sort of dejection. A misunderstanding could never have been any bigger.

6

It's raining hard. It always rains hard in Germany. I reach the Ettinger Street bus stop and wait there for bus No. 70. The street looks bedraggled. Streams of murky water wash away the spit and cigarette butts flung around by people.

The tall building on the opposite side of the street attracts my attention. An ugly one, painted in a gloomy grey, with an old, dusty scaffold staircase in front, leading up to the roof.

A cool, invigorating breeze keeps blowing, pumping fresh air into the town.

The bus arrives. I get on. The bus driver's listless face is a quick reminder of the bleak moments I had today. I say "Guten Tag" which means "good day." He just nods. I find my way through the people standing and finally manage to lean to the large window in the middle of the bus.

My trousers and cap are soaked through. I feel cold. I try to find some tissues in my pockets to dry up my forehead. It's useless. They're all wet.

I look through the window and contemplate the murky sky, filled with dark grey clouds looking like insidious monsters. I think for a moment how sad it is. How sad it is that I know that these monsters are only huge piles of condensed vapor hanging around. How sad it is that I can't enjoy the bliss of some fantasy, some illusion. Why should science disenchant me like this? Why, in these precarious moments of my life I can't even delude myself into some reverie?

All of a sudden, the sound of an old woman brings me back to the present tense.

"Darf ich bitte aussteigen Junger Mann?" which means, "May I please get out, young man?" she says while she looks annoyed as I've blocked her way to the exit door.

"Sorry," I answer and make room for her to walk out. She frowns and passes past me. "These young people, these young people," she complains as she leaves the bus.

I reach my house which is located at Hollerstaude. This is simply the name of a district in Düsseldorf. I scurry towards the front door. Suddenly, the mewing of a very small, white cat attracts my attention. It is crouching under a bush, its fur soggy.

"Hi little cutesy pussy," I say.

The poor cat looks weak and frail. I can hardly hear its voice. It looks into my eyes through its slit-like pupils. Suddenly I have a weird feeling. It is as if this cat and me have everything in common in the universe. As if we've known each other for ages. As if only it can understand my predicament and only I know how it feels now under this dripping foliage. At first I want to take it inside with me. But then I reverse my decision.

"Sorry small cat, I can't take you inside. You know I'm not having a good day. I hope you will forgive me." I say slowly, like I do when I speak to foreigners, as if the small cat would understand my words in German if I talk more slowly. It doesn't look at me anymore. I take pity on it, but I can't cause myself more trouble at this moment. I leave it behind...

I enter the building and go up the stairs and enter my room. I walk into the bath-room in search for a towel. Suddenly, the doorbell rings.

"I'll be right there," I shout out of the bathroom as I wrap the smaller towel around my head. I look in the mirror, it looks terrible. The doorbell rings again.

"Shit! Why these people don't leave me in peace," I mumble as I deem there's again my old lady neighbor at the door wanting to complain about last night's loud music. I run to the door and open up. It's my landlord, Mr. Jacobson, a tall blond guy with striking blue eyes. He looks great, but he's not. He's a greedy and sometimes boorish person who owns tens of apartments. I never forget the long discussion we had once on who will pay the garbage collection fee, which was only €60 per year back then. He gave up only when I threatened I would sue him for a breach of con-tract.

I wonder what he is doing here. To my surprise, he talks kindly and warmly:

"Hi Mr. Armin, I wanted to ask you if you could come over to my place tomorrow evening, around 8:00 PM. We're having a feast," he says addressing me as always with my first name Armin as he can't pronounce my family name Zeitzer correctly.

I think for a short moment that the world is not as calamitous as I sometimes deem. I suddenly think of Natalie, who was so kind to me today. He continues:

"Would you like to come? I'll be very glad if you accept."

"Yes, I will. Thank you!" I reply and then ask, "Is there any especial reason for you party?"

"You'll know," he answers laughingly, "Well see you tomorrow, Mr. Armin!"

He walks off down the stairs. I say goodbye and shut the door. I go into the bath-room and take a shower. It's really pleasant after a long day having been outside in the cold. I make some hot tea, sit at my desk and turn on the PC in order to work on a story I'm writing in German. I get absorbed in it, quite deliberately, in order to for-get my dire situation. All of a sudden, the vision of the small cat appears in my mind's eye. I feel a chill in my heart. I try to think of something else. I take the last letter I've got from the university administration out of its envelope, maybe with hope that its contents have been somehow changed, by some wonder. It reads the same as the last one hundred times that I've read it:

"Dear Mr. Zeitzer, we regret having to inform you that your application for a scholarship has been rejected by the office of dean, we hope you otherwise the best in your life."

I crumple and throw it to a side. I look at the cup of tea. Whiffs of vapor are leaving its surface, making me wonder how come the water inside does not decrease quickly. I contemplate that surface for a while, but suddenly the vision of the small cat appears before my eyes again. I can't bear it any longer. I put on my overcoat and cap and go down the stairs and then outside. I search under the bush I saw the cat before. It's not there anymore...

Ω Ω Ω

I'm preparing myself for the so called feast as my landlord said yesterday. I dress in a suit my father once gave me. It looks quite new, however, and by no means old-fashioned. My thoughts are as ridiculous as they can be. I think it's anyway a positive thing to eat at his place, because I can save the money for one portion. It's quite cold outside. As soon as I leave the building's door I see the bush of yesterday. I feel a chill in my heart and scurry away.

At Mr. Jacobson's place, I sit at a long table they've prepared for their meal inside. I ask Melanie, Mr. Jacobson's girlfriend if she needs help with setting the table.

"No Armin. You can help yourself later with the meal. There, you see the table over there?" she points to a table near to the huge window beside the terrace.

I've been here before. I had to feed their cat, called Mitsi (in German written Mitzi) several times when they went on holidays. It's not a huge house, especially for a wealthy man like Mr. Jacobson who owns several houses and many apartments. It's the German culture. We remain economical even if we're very rich.

All of a sudden, the voice of a woman sitting already beside me brings me back to the present tense.

"Hello," she says, "who are you?"

9

I look up to her. I suddenly feel a startle in my heart.

She is blond, an attractive woman in her mid-thirties. She has blue eyes, a tall forehead, regular lineaments, and wears a sexy tank top accentuating her curvy breasts.

"What are you looking at?" she asks the next moment with a bit irritated tone.

"Oh I'm sorry, hi, my name is Armin," I answer as I try to pull my sight off that beautiful bust.

She laughs and gives an affected smile.

"My name is Deborah," she says.

"Deborah? Are you American or British?" I ask.

"No, I'm German. Haven't you heard such a name in Germany so far?" she asks.

"Never," I answer.

"No, there are other Deborahs in Germany, believe me!" she says as she fills her goblet with red wine and offers me some. "May I help you?" she asks.

"Sure, thanks!" I reply as I move my glass towards her so that she can fill it up. I keep looking at her beautiful mien. She notices that she's in the center of my focus but she plays dumb. Then, she squints and looks as if she's very curious about some-thing but doesn't dare ask it. However, she finally blurts it out:

"So are you born in Germany? You look rather like French, or Italian," she says.

"Yes, in Ingolstadt, to a Maltese mother, and a German father," I answer calmly.

"Ingolstadt is a small town, isn't it?" she says.

"Much smaller than Düsseldorf," I say, and then, after a short pause, I continue, "but it's funny that actually a Stadt (German word for city) is much smaller than a Dorf (German word for village) in reality, isn't it?"

She thinks for a short a while and then as a grin appears on her blossom like lips, she says, "Oh you mean Dorf at the end of Düsseldorf?! You're smart!"

Suddenly Mr. Jacobson asks anyone to be silent. And then he takes Melanie by the hand to the front of the long table at which we're sitting.

"Attention please! Everybody attention please!" he calls out with a face shining with happiness, the one I've seldom seen on him.

"I'd like to announce that I and Melanie have married last week. And next week, we'll have our honeymoon in Mallorca," he says. Everyone cheers while his sister looks astonished, "What do you mean?" she shouts confusedly, "shouldn't I know this?! Does mother know it?"

It seems like the sister is somewhat angry, but I don't follow their discussion any-more. Instead, I turn my attention to Deborah.

What a beautiful name! Deborah. I remember I saw this name for the first time in a Time magazine of my father's. I remember it was an article about an actress, a beautiful American actress called Deborah Raffin I surmise. She was tall and thin, and as I recollect I saw her in a photo in the article as she was getting on a truck.

And this German Deborah. I wonder for a moment how can a human being be so beautiful? How is it possible? Is she beautiful because I think she's beautiful? Be-cause she's a woman and I'm a male fellow human who's ready and willing to mate? Would an alien find her adorable too?

Crazy theories propagate through my mind. Why are German women so sexy? I recently read in a scientific journal called Spektrum der Wissenschaft (in English: The Spectrum of Science) that blond people with blue eyes were created for the first time through mutation in a couple of genes some 10,000 years ago. In that time the world climate and nature landscape were very different from now. Icy temperatures pre-vailed over most of the European continent, especially northern parts. This made survival for humans very difficult, forcing men to mate with only one woman and to provide her with food and shelter, as women couldn't hunt prey as effectively as men. Back then natural selection was based on the woman's beauty, therefore women having darker hair and eyes slowly vanished giving way to blond women. This changed the whole ethnic landscape of North Europe. However, this never means women in other parts of the world are ugly. In Far East the same natural selection was in favor of slit-eyed folks. There men found women with narrower eyes more beautiful. Therefore, they sustained them preferably, forgetting the rest. That's to say beauty lies in the eye of the beholder, as the saying goes. Moreover, beauty is the result of harsh life for the women who ceased to survive for the prettier to get by. It can therefore be considered as an effective weapon, like a keen sword.

"So what do you do?" Deborah's delicate voice pushes my thoughts out of my mind.

"I'm a student, a bachelor student at Düsseldorf University," I reply.

"What do you study?"

"Electrical engineering," I reply, "What do you do?" I now dare to ask as she's al-ready asked about me.

"I'm a model, and in addition I run a private business," she replies.

I'm surprised. "What? What do you mean exactly with being a model?" I immediately ask.

"You don't know what a model does? Like I pose for Madlen furniture, for Inmozer (she means another furniture retailer active in Germany), for Mim (a clothes retailer) and so on, in their advertisement brochures," she replies.

I blush. She's a model and I'm just an engineering student. Sheesh! I remember that even that is not for sure anymore. I've already run out of money, and I'll soon have to give up studying in case no one helps. I heave a deep sigh and look at the stars. The day has already given way to the night, and the clear sky reveals its truth to the inhabitants of Earth. My eyes search for Venus, my favorite celestial body. The planet brightest in the night, next to the moon.

"Are you sad?" she asks me shortly after.

As if I suddenly deeply trust her I tell her about my sordid fortunes. But I try to speak low because I don't want that my landlord hears what I say.

"Yes, I have no money," I reply as my eyes turn watery.

"I see. You poor thing," she says, "Why don't you ask your parents for help?"

"Well my father doesn't care, and my mother isn't available to me," I answer.

"What do you mean she isn't available? Where is she? Is she in Germany?"

"She's just not available," I say and pause to evade any other questions about my mother.

"Sorry! I didn't want to be nosy," she says.

I smile and say, "No problem. You didn't say anything wrong. I just don't feel comfortable to talk about my mother. It has its own reasons."

Suddenly an old lady sitting on the opposite of us at the table interrupts. She asks Deborah about her plans to open up an own fashion shop in Cologne, a city near to Düsseldorf. I don't follow their conversation. I get absorbed again in my fantasies. I think how simple the life could be if I would be a slave to this woman instead of studying at university. I could do her housework, wash up her dishes, and shop for her. In that case I'd have a much calmer, more stable life. I envy the people who've lived in the past. In those past days being a slave was nothing to be ashamed of.

All of a sudden, her voice addressing me brings me back to the present tense. I'm so excited that she cares about me, that she hasn't forgotten that I'm sitting there, beside her.

"So why don't you apply for BAföG?" she asks.

"They rejected my application. They said because my father can afford supporting me I'm not eligible to get BAFöG."

Her eyes open wide as she makes a surprised face. She says, "Wow!! And your father does not want to support?!"

"Nope," I answer as I blink and feel ashamed. But then I pull myself together and say with a bit more self-confidence, "But I'm sure I'll find a way."

She rolls her eyes. She looks at the half-filled glass of wine in front of her and traces its rim with her delicate, beautiful fingers. Then she says:

"Why don't you search for a job?"

"I'm searching," I answer, "but I haven't found anything yet. You know I wished I weren't studying engineering here in Düsseldorf. In Stuttgart or Munich it's much easier to find engineering related student jobs. In Düsseldorf there's nothing. Here is better for ones who study finance or economics. And it's hard to find a job in a restaurant or something, and even if I could it doesn't pay off."

"What do you know other than engineering?" she asks.

"I know very well English, and French," I answer.

"That's pretty impressive, but that wouldn't help that much."

"I also know accounting. I worked as an accountant in my father's company. He taught it to me. He is an accountant. I also have an accounting certificate," I said.

Suddenly her eyes show more enthusiasm, but then for some reason, she holds back. She looks at the old woman again and asks how she finds the wine being served here.

The old woman smiles the way a typical, polite older German woman does and says, "nicht Schlecht!" which means not bad. Deborah turns her face to me. She says:

"Listen! I have a small start-up company where I design fashion and new dresses for women. So far I'm doing the accounting on my own. However, you could help me there, and maybe also negotiate with some clients in Britain as you say your English is pretty good," she says.

I rejoice in my heart. I can't believe someone, some stranger, wants to help me like this. I want to kiss her hand, no, I would rather kiss her feet. "Hooray!" I shout in my heart.

"Thanks a lot," I say with a huge smile on my face.

Ω Ω Ω

I've been working in Deborah's company for two weeks now. I sit in a small of-fice beside the room where Deborah designs new dresses. She's shown me some of her works and although I'm not a woman and have no clue about women's fashion, I'm quite impressed by her creativity.

The accounting system she runs here is very different from what I know from my father's bolt producing company. She uses a software she's bought at Amazon for €10 or so, whereas at my father's company I filled out an account-book with figures. However, I've already figured out how to work out the accounts.

I think about my steamy chat on WhatsApp with Deborah last night. It's strange how new media like WhatsApp and Facebook have changed the way we communicate with people around us. No wonder it's claimed that today Facebook is responsible for one third of separations worldwide.

It all began with a small comment of hers on WhatsApp:

"By the way, Armin! Would you mind dressing more formally at work. Today you looked too casual. You know we're not working in a factory. I'd like to be held in esteem by visitors and clients."

"Oh I'm sorry! I have to buy a new suit then," I wrote back.

"But you have already a good suit. The one you wore on the wedding party at Jacobson's. The grey one. I like it."

"Oh no! That one?! It's so old. There's a secret about it."

"What secret?"

"No I think it's better that I'll buy a new one."

"What secret?! Tell me."

I first held back from answering. I am young but I've already gone through enough troubles to know that I shouldn't become very chummy with my employer, even if she's a beautiful, sexy woman. However, I deemed in this case telling the truth would not harm me. I answered:

"It belonged to my father!"

"Lol!" she answered with lots of laughing emoticons. The ones the small yellow face guffaws and sheds tears of joy at once. I felt ashamed. But shortly after, she wrote back:

"No Armin believe me. It doesn't look old at all. You looked really hot in it."

This sentence spurred my sensation up to the hilt. My heart was beating so fast it could burst out of my chest any time. I forgot every rule of etiquette altogether. I wrote back with an honesty I'd seldom known of myself:

"Deborah, when you were sitting there, I thought how can a human being be so beautiful? How can it be possible? Your blue eyes, your blond locks of hair, your magnificent figure. I wondered if you're a human being or an angel..."

She wrote back surprisingly fast. WhatsApp was showing "Deborah is typing" for a while on top of the interface screen. It felt as if hours went by, although it was only perhaps a minute or so.

"I may look like an angel. But I have a small devil deep inside."

I couldn't believe she was talking to me like this. When a woman discloses her nasty secrets to a man, she trusts him already to a good extent.

"I'd like to get to know that small devil. I would do anything for it," I wrote back.

She didn't reply.

Ω Ω Ω

Deborah enters my small office with a big smile. She paces the room up and down several time and says, "Guess what Armin! I have a huge contract now, with a famous British dress retailer!"

"That sounds great!" I say, "Congratulations!" I stand up to shake hands with her. I feel as if I'm someone important in her life. We press each other's hands. But when I want to let go of it, she holds on. She presses more. I'm confused. She gazes into my eyes. Then, she pushes me back onto my chair, and sits on my desk, on the mass of small papers and notes I'm working out. She talks slowly, with eyes full of desire:

"Do I look like an angel today?"

"Yes, my dear," I answer as I breathe hard. My hands are shivering. It's so embarrassing.

She bows down and kisses my lips. I'm dumbfounded. I want to kiss her longer, but she moves back. She holds up her skirt. I can see her beautiful black slip.

"Do you want to take it off?" she whispers.

"More than anything!" I answer.

"Go on!"

I help her strip off that slip. I can see her shaved pussy. Tears of joy well up in my eyes. "It's so beautiful!" I say, "How can you be so beautiful even there?" I say while I almost want to shed tears of happiness.

She smiles. She doesn't say anything. She grabs a bunch of my hair and pushes my face onto her pussy. "Stick your tongue inside, as far as you can," she says with a shaking voice.

I do my best to please her. I'm in disbelief the whole time. How can such a wonderful thing happen?! Is this real, or am I only dreaming? I feel her pussy lips swell in my mouth. It's so exciting! I can feel them throb. I put my hand on her breast with the excuse to knead it, but actually to feel her heart beating. The harmonious throbbing and beating is one of the best melodies I've ever savored in my life.

Deborah moans hard and loud. We hold each other's hands in that moment. It's so beautiful! So exciting!

16

Tonight I'm so happy in my heart. I feel like I was born again today. I feel like I'm a small child who's found an exciting new toy. I sing the poem I read once in a short stories book as I cook meatballs. It's a translation from Persian into English by Kinga Markus in a book my mother once gave me as a gift for my birthday. I think I was eleven back then:

"The night was gone, and came the morn;

My glorious lucky day has been born!

The sun, the king of stars as yet

Has not raised to the sky his head,

When I open my sleepy eyes

To hail the sun as he doth rise…

To hear my father's kindly words,

Sweet whispers from my mother,

I open up my sleepy eyes

To hail the sun as he doth rise."

It reminds me of a very kind, attractive English teacher I had back in school, Ms. Christina Dengel. She had green eyes, an oval face, and brown curly hair reaching her shoulders. I remember when she once asked if anyone in the class could recite an English poem. I immediately stretched out my hand excitedly, went to the front of the class upon her beckon, closed my eyes and sang it loud.

I was very proud in that moment. I forgot that my father had smacked and scolded me that morning saying, "You're a scatterbrained bum fit for nothing."

At the end, I turned red as I was a bit coy back then. However, I can't forget how Ms. Dengel's eyes were radiating with admiration. "Bravo Armin!" she said as the whole class clapped their hands.

Suddenly, my smartphone buzzing brings me back to reality. I look at the screen. I've got a message from someone whom I don't know! I wash my hands with soap and water and read the message.

17

"Dear Armin, I'm sorry for what happened today. I hope you're not angry with me. I was so excited about the contract with the guys in England. I just wanted to vent my feelings. You were there. I remembered our conversation last night. I know that it went awry," it reads.

I'm confused. This should be Deborah, but why is she writing me with a covert ac-count?

I answer:

"No problem! I remember our conversation. Actually I enjoyed what happened today!"

"Yes maybe. But I think we shouldn't repeat it."

I think for a while and imagine those beautiful moments. As if I lose control over my hand, I punch in:

"Do you want to know what I dreamed last night?"

"What?"

"I dreamed that I was a farmer around Jerusalem in medieval times, and that you were part of a crusader battalion attacking our neighborhood. You saw me and took me with yourself as a slave, your own slave."

"I'm happy that we don't live in those times any more. I hate wars. I might have got angry at you and have even killed you out of petty reasons."

"But that would have been ok!" I answer.

"What? Why?"

"I would love to die for you."

For a while she doesn't answer. I'm so excited that I can't continue with cooking anymore. My heart beats so hard I feel all veins on my entire body throbbing. Shortly after she writes:

"Literally?"

This single word knocks my socks off. What does she mean with this? Does she really want me to die for her? I am so excited. I would, I really would! After a short time, I don't know why, but as if I have to reply to her every single question I write an answer. I don't care if she would hold me for the dumbest person on

Earth, or if she thinks that as I'm alone now, and my family doesn't care about me, I'm vulnerable and am a sitting duck, and she could do anything she'd like to me.

"Yes," I write in response, "and I mean it!"

Ω Ω Ω

Today at work the history repeats itself after a short time. Deborah suddenly enters my small office looking livid. She puts her hands on her waist and stares at me. A weird silence prevails in the room for several moments.

First I don't dare say anything. But then, partly in order to break the dreadful silence I ask her:

"Deborah, could I ask you something?"

"What's that?"

"I've run out of money. I'm broke. Could you lend me some money before my first salary at the end of this month? I'll give it back as soon as I have the salary."

"Do I look like your mother?" she retorts, "You'll get your salary at the end of the month."

I'm in shock. It's confusing. She knows that I would die for her but she abstains from lending me several hundred Euros. I don't react. She walks to me slowly. She doesn't kiss me this time. She sits on the desk again. She looks at me with furious eyes, as if I've done something wrong. "Go down on me!" she says in a tone so patronizing that it reminds me of my father.

I pull her skirt and panties down slowly. I look at her face. She still looks angry.

"Is everything all right?" I dare to ask again.

"Oh, don't talk so much. Do it!" She answers.

She isn't shaved today. I bow my head and go for her clit. I flick against it with my tongue. I then begin licking the pussy lips gently and try to enjoy it as far as I can. I think she's probably had a bad day, that's why she's speaking with me in this unkind tone.

"I don't feel anything! What are you doing?" she says.

Before I say anything she lets out a hiss of anger and this time she almost yells at me, "Can't you do it right?! Lick it right! No, stick your tongue inside. Didn't you get me?"

I pull the skin around her cunt apart and stick my tongue inside. I try to tongue-fuck her. At this time, I remember a sentence my father said when we were on a tour in Vienna (we Germans call it Wien), Austria. We were promenading around in the castle of Schönbrunn, a former imperial summer residence which belonged to Austrian emperors. In one of the gardens we saw a sculpture figuring a royal family, including a beautiful woman in regal attire, perhaps an empress, riding on the back of a poor, sordid vassal clothed in rags.

"Look at this son! Pure reality depicted in a statue. This is what I call honest art, a masterpiece!" he said.

Ω Ω Ω

Tonight I feel a bit strange.

However, I deem many would wish to be in my shoes, to lick a beautiful princess in her most intimate spots.

I think of other things for now. I've bought eggplants and am pouring some salt on it. My mother once told this way all nocuous material inside its flesh would be absorbed out and one could enjoy the remaining delicious portion. I'm cooking a Maltese dish.

Suddenly my smartphone buzzes. I look. It's Deborah. She's written:

"I'm so sorry for what happened today, Armin! You know the client in England has cancelled his order, out of some weird reason. I was very angry. I had to give a vent to my fury. Sorry! I really didn't want to wreak it on you. I saw you… I'm so sorry Armin!"

I write back, "No problem. I understand."

I lean my smartphone upwards to a cupboard in my kitchen to see if she writes back while I cook. She doesn't. I then take the smartphone again in my hand and write:

"Don't worry about me dear Deborah! I'm ok. I know that you've probably had a bad day. And I enjoyed the way you treated me today."

She writes back: "Are you being serious?"

20

"Don't worry. Nothing has happened. I should apologize. I asked for salary too early. What you did wasn't that bad. Please don't feel sorrow or remorse about it. I don't want that you suffer."

She doesn't reply.

I read my own reply on WhatsApp screen and have to laugh about my own foolishness. How can I apologize while she's been so harsh to me?

Ω Ω Ω

However, now that I'm writing this story, and am much older, I know why:

I once read in a novel that once two people meet one of them automatically turns into the other one's slave. I think even today this holds true for every relationship to some extent. You can see it in everyday life. No interaction between people is perfectly fair. In corporations people are slave to their bosses, working tooth and nail and earning less and less with passing time. In families there are mostly two kinds of hierarchical systems: Patriarchy or matriarchy, at least this is what I know from my acquaintances and friends.

Ω Ω Ω

I think if my mother were here she would certainly be very proud of her son. The eggplant stew, containing also some lamb meat and chickpeas, tastes wonderful.

I miss her so much!

And I'm happy everything went well. I'm happy Deborah will not burn in remorse tonight.

Ω Ω Ω

Here I'm again, in my small office. I try to work out and fix the bugs I encountered yesterday while fitting the accounts. As I've lost myself in the beauty and power of figures and mathematics, Deborah enters my room unexpectedly as usual.

She's wearing a short skirt which shows off her beautiful, spotless white skin. Like always she sits on the desk and she puts one leg on the other. She's outlined her beautiful eyes in black, accentuating the beautiful contrast between her dark whimpers and her ocean blue eyes, and has put on a rosy lipstick. To me she looks like a female deity, in no uncertain terms.

21

I remember the cartoon Itchy and Scratchy played once in a while in the animated TV series The Simpsons, the American cartoon very popular in Germany. I loved to watch it on the ProSieben Channel. There the poor hapless cat is repeatedly maimed and killed by the sadistic blue mouse, but the dumb cat falls for the mouse's tricks and lies over and over again. I feel like I've fallen in love anew, in this endless, divine beauty. I put my hand on her thigh and she puts hers on it. Then she moves my hand away. She smiles and says:

"You need to finish the accounts till tomorrow evening. The tax inspector will be here tomorrow. Can you manage it?"

"Sure," I say as I breathe hard and fast, my heart brimful with fervent desire.

"Perfect!" she says. Then she puts her hand on my hair and strokes it a bit. Shortly after, while she gazes into my eyes, she says, "What are you doing this weekend?"

"I haven't planned anything especial. Why do you ask?"

"I can invite you to dinner. Do you have time? On Saturday?" she says.

"Great! I know a good Greek restaurant..." I say but she cuts me off, "No, I know already where we shall go. Ibis hotel."

I'm surprised. Ibis hotel is a hotel, not a restaurant! However, I resign to her will.

"All right!" I answer.

Ω Ω Ω

I wonder why we've come here. I never imagined that I would once opt for a hotel to have dinner. Anyway, I'm very thankful to Deborah because she's going to pay. We've had delicious spaetzle, a specialty from Southern Germany made by boiling small lumps of dough which are in turn made from flour and eggs. It's particularly popular in Swabian regions of Baden-Württemberg, the area around Stuttgart I mean.

"You're very lucky young man!" says the waiter, "your girlfriend is so beautiful, and still, she's paying."

I don't know if he's being serious or it's supposed to be a quip. I feel ashamed anyway. I don't raise my head to look at him.

"Don't be sad," Deborah says while she touches my hand.

"I'm not sad!" I reply, "Someday I will make up for this. Someday I'll be rich and will invite you to a dinner, in a very expensive and luxurious restaurant," I say with a heart full of hope.

"I've booked a room for tonight, for the two of us, here!" she says.

"What? Why here? Why not at my place, or at yours? I still don't know where you live. Where do you live?" I ask lots of questions at once.

"Well, the beds here are good. Their better than the ones in my place, and certainly better than what we could find at yours," she replies.

Her answer sounds weird. I'm hesitant. Why here?

We make our way upstairs. She takes me by the hand.

We enter the small, economically designed room with a huge bed in the middle. Deborah goes into the bathroom but comes back at once. She smiles at me and strokes my arm.

"Don't worry! You won't die tonight!" she says.

She hugs and kisses me. I'm so excited. It feels as if my Goddess is endowing me with care and mercy. It's beautiful to be in her arms!

She then whispers softly in my ear:

"Take your clothes off and lie on the bed, my Armin!"

My heart is palpitating. I'm so happy, so honored. The phrase "My Armin" reverberates in my head a thousand times. I disrobe and lie on the bed. My beautiful Deborah does the same, slowly. And then she lies beside me. She kisses me on the cheek, and says:

"Will you give me head again? I'm so horny!"

I'm so excited. I unbutton her blouse with a speed I'd never known of myself. Then I hastily open up her fly and unzip her trousers. I could hear her panting hard.

As soon as her trousers are off, her flawless, soft skin reveals under the lustrous light of the tiny hotel room. My heart is so filled with cheer that it's going to explode. I take her panties off and then eye the beauty I don't want to miss the slightest of. My heart misses a beat when she says, "Go on! What are you waiting for? Eat me out!"

23

I lick her pussy lips and clit and knead her thighs and groin with my both hands. She's moaning hard and loud. Shortly after, she says, "Take off your clothes. Put your penis in me!"

Ω Ω Ω

We're doing it for half an hour now, with me alternately thrusting my penis and licking her nipples and at times her juicy pussy. My lips are completely wet, not out of my own saliva, but from her abundant juices.

When she has hers, she groans loud and scratches my back skin with her sharp, manicured fingernails. I immediately go down on her and continue to lick her in every corner. But suddenly, a vague notion passes through my mind and wrings my heart. Tears well up in my eyes and run down my cheeks. I try to choke them back, but to no avail. Deborah notices.

"What's happened? Why are you so sad?"

"Nothing, everything is fine! Everything is great!"

"Come on! Tell me, tell me! Armin!"

"No forget it! Let it be. Could you please part your legs farther that I can lick easier?"

"No I won't. Tell me what's wrong?!"

My voice is shaking. I want to sob but I hold back. Then, I close my eyes and say, "I just thought for a moment, for a short moment, that how sad it is, that this beautiful thing that we have, is not forever. You know, we don't have a relationship. I'm not your boyfriend. Maybe we sleep together a couple of times, but then? What about then?"

Deborah lets out a hiss of annoyance and then takes a deep sigh, "O, Armin! I'm much older than you. It's not right. We can't have a relationship."

"Is that it? Or is it just an excuse? Because I'm not rich, nor successful?" I say with a voice still trembling.

"No, no! Don't do this to me, you're ruining our beautiful night!" she says, and then after a short pause she continues, "I think it's better that I put on my clothes and go."

"No, no! Please no. I'm sorry! I promise I won't utter a word again."

She's right. I was going to ruin everything with blurting out that nonsense. I grab her hand and hold it firmly. I kiss it…

I am lucky! She doesn't pull back!

I lead her again to the middle of the bed and help her part her legs. And shortly after, I am licking that delicious pussy another time around. However, that notion lingers in my mind. I feel sorry for myself. The only thing that heartens me is Deborah's pleasant moaning.

Ω Ω Ω

I open my eyes. I feel dizzy. I still lie flat on bed in the hotel room. Deborah has left apparently. I try to make it to the shelf beside the window, where I've put my ID and smartphone. It is twilight outside. I look at the smartphone screen. It reads 8:00 A.M.

I leave the room and go down the stairs. The receptionist lady, a plump blond woman wearing glasses, doesn't even notice my presence. She's reading a Bild news-paper portraying a beautiful, stark naked model on its back page.

"Hi, I've spent last night in room D 14. Has my partner already paid for the room?" I ask. She looks at me from under her glasses with glazed eyes, heavy and dull.

"Your girlfriend has paid the room," she replies and immediately looks into the mass of papers in her hands again.

I leave the hotel lobby and walk toward where I'd locked up my bicycle. I unfasten the lock and get on. I feel hungry. Figures of a bag of Alnatura muesli and a pocket of delicious milk dance in my mind's eye. I ride towards the Lidl hypermarket on my way home.

I'm glad at seeing Alnatura chocolate muesli available. My day gets better, bit by bit, step by step.

I ride home relishing the reminiscence of what happened last night. At the entrance I hear the sound of a cat or something from under the bush. My whole body trembles. My hand quivers. I stoop down. I see a small, white cat lying there. Although it's not raining, dripping from the bush foliage has made it wet. I stretch out my hand and grab it. I take it with me.

I enter my apartment. I momentarily put the small cat on the ground. I shut the door behind me. I take the cat to the bathroom and unroll some toilet paper to dry it up. I then blow over it with the blow-dryer and take it to the living room.

I see my father calling me on the smartphone. I reject the call. I pour some milk into a bowl for the small cat to drink and wait to see if it can lap milk. After a minute or so, it does!

$$\Omega \quad \Omega \quad \Omega$$

My small cat looks content. I hug it in my tight embrace. I don't care how ridiculous we two look now. An unshaved man holding a small cat in his arms. It should look very funny!

Suddenly, the smartphone buzzes again. Deborah has written something. I tap on the screen to see her message:

"Dear Armin! Thanks for the last night. Sorry I had to leave early. I didn't want to wake you up at the weekend. Don't worry, last night won't be our last time."

My heart beats fast. I hold the cat even tighter.

We both watch through the window as the sky clears from clouds. I feel happy in my heart. I think the small cat too. It has a sort of sparkle in its eyes.

I whisper in its ear:

"The night was gone, and came the morn;

My glorious lucky day has been born!

The sun, the king of stars as yet

Has not raised to the sky his head,

When I open my sleepy eyes

To hail the sun as he doth rise...

To hear my father's kindly words,

Sweet whispers from my mother,

I open up my sleepy eyes

To hail the sun as he doth rise."

When an Angel Shivers

I was still a child my mother used to say. Same thing that woman told me in the nightclub, but it didn't keep her from rubbing her body to mine as we danced. I think she was thirty or something. "Touch me," she said. I had knocked back several bottles of blonde beer, so her words prompted me to get impudent and grab her hip. Her eyes shone with consent as she brought her busty body still closer to mine and whispered, "Touch the middle." I got excited. My ears were on fire. Her face had flushed. I was still wary. Had I heard it right? There in the middle of a discotheque among one hundred people who danced around wildly you would have felt free, but by nature I was always cautious. She however turned out to be impatient. She grabbed my hand and slipped it toward her gooch. My heart was going to explode. My middle finger all but pierced her jeans. She moaned and flung her arms around my neck. I hugged her tight and smelled the aroma of her body. We danced, necked and kissed, and later, in my small bed in the student dormitory, we knocked ourselves out.

Ω Ω Ω

We Germans are famous for being liberal in our relationships, but I tell you this fame is by a large part an exaggeration. It is limited to late hours in a nightclub, or on huge parties such as the world famous October Festival in Munich where we drink lots of beer. We call it the 'Oktoberfest.' Otherwise a German man almost always ends up, after at most a few years of single life, attached to a woman like glue, or he makes a woman pregnant and so he's attached to a whole family right from the beginning. There are many reasons for that. One is that Germans love family and many men love to have and raise children. But there are other important reasons as well, and one is what makes my heart palpitate and my dick make a tiny move even when I only articulate or write the sentence, "GERMAN WOMEN ARE SEXY!!!" Oh yes. You don't agree?! So let's put it in another way. Just consider you meet a tall girl with oval face, green eyes, smooth skin, a dainty nose, leggy, and a tiny belly. Would you say you've met a woman or rather an angel? Every time I meet another woman I try to mention this at least once to her, that I am honored to meet an angel. And alas, to make it short, one of these irresistible angels ended my singleness quite early on at the university where I studied for a bachelor of Organic Chemistry in the city of Düsseldorf in West Germany.

Well I want to give you some background about this city and why I ended there. Düsseldorf is a large city, with almost I guess a million inhabitants. The famous Rhine River snakes through it and parts it into old and modern parts.

All in all, I find Düsseldorf not a picturesque beauty. It's not because I was born in the rivaling city of Cologne which is just a few miles away, but because I have been to many places and towns across Europe, from Nuremberg in Germany itself to Lisbon, the fascinating capital of Portugal and am thus travelled enough to assure you that in the beautiful Europe seldom would you stumble upon a town as mundane as Düsseldorf. Were it not for the mere relatively high population of this city, I am sure even I would have never bothered to move even that distance of a few miles to wind up there.

Yes, and in this city I went to university, because my hometown was only a couple of minutes away with the regional train. Well, if I grew homesick all I needed was to take the next train and arrive at my city of origin moments later. However, no matter how much I admired my mother for her magnificent cooking skills and her expertise to regale you sumptuously with traditional German cuisine, the appeal of independence and freedom of my parents' comments on every trivial matter of my life was strong enough to rent a small room in the students dormitory on the Schiller street in Düsseldorf. I paid only two hundred euros per month. God I still can't believe it myself when I say the number, 200 euros. For those of you who are not European 200 euros is something like 220 American dollars. I had a room for myself, and shared a kitchen, two bathrooms and two showers with only ten other students. Nowadays you could never find accommodation so cheap, not in Düsseldorf, not in Germany, not even in Europe. I pine over the memories of those past days. How happy I was! Why happy? I forgot to say, during the time when I was single every weekend, of course with the exception of the exam period, my small single bed was where women from many different social strata slept in my arms, or conversely I slept in their arms. Lawyers, teachers, cooks, even one singer are on my proud portfolio.

I listened to their stories, and most were sad ones. Women complaining about ex-husbands having abused them or having been unfair with the alimony after divorce, about having to bring up children on their own, problems at work and the ever present discrimination of women who although are at least as qualified as their fellow male colleagues, almost always earn less money. I once even met a female CEO of a large company who told a story about one of her business trips to Switzerland. Did you know that beautiful Switzerland is the worst country in Europe as to gender gap? They let their women vote for the first time only in 1971. Can you imagine?! In the heart of Europe Swiss women hadn't had the right to take part in federal elections until 1971! And there in Appenzell Innerrhoden canton not until 1991!

Anyway that CEO-I think she was in her mid-forties but still sexy and with large hips but quite leggy-told me how in Switzerland the staff of the company where she visited had thought she'd been in fact the secretary of the CEO of her own company and had asked her when that gentleman would arrive? She was upset and felt disparaged and couldn't concentrate for a while during the presentation she'd prepared with so much endeavor, and had wanted to sob in tears but had to hold back to pull off the deal. She was a wonderful charismatic woman, with a little too sour slit however. Maybe that was because as a manager she was often as not under huge stress. That would make the female genitalia sour I guess. Or maybe she hadn't taken a shower that day, but I doubt that because she didn't smell of sweet and when I sucked her nipples they weren't salty. So I gave her a long head to compensate for all the trouble my Swiss fellow males had caused the hapless attractive and successful woman to go through. She was kind to me! A large part of the time when I was eating her juicy pussy she played with my hair and caressed it. Maybe she had grown to have motherly affections for me. Back in the nightclub she'd told me I'd been almost her son's age.

Anyway as we Germans say, "Lange Rede, kurzer Sinn" or as British say "to cut a long story short" I was busy eating out every sort of woman until one day, when I had gone to study and prepare for the exam of Physical Chemistry in the library of university I saw a young girl, even younger than me, sitting opposite me with a distance of a few meters at the other side of a long library desk. Have I already told you how an angel looks like? Tall and leggy, a short skirt, an oval face with a pointed noise and green eyes, and a blond ponytail bundled on the back of her hair. She was but an angel with glasses, which made her still more beautiful, as they magnified her pretty eyes and so she looked so gorgeous that if I had seen her in a club beside a boy with a sturdy build who I'd deemed her boyfriend, I would have still gone up to her to ask if she would like something to drink and needed someone to invite her. Probably that fictional boy would have broken all my teeth in my mouth after that. But now, I was there, with an angel-looking girl who had landed near me, without any rivaling boy around, and my heart throbbed as fast as my dick. But still I didn't dare go to her. Why? I don't know. At one moment she looked at me with strange eyes as if to say, "What are you looking at?" and I swiftly opened the thick book of Physical Chemistry in front of me and made as if losing myself in the passion of love for science, whereas it was my heart that experienced passion then. I didn't dare look at her again, and later on quite surprisingly got so concentrated on reading that confusing course material that I didn't notice when she'd left the desk again. Why was she gone? Did she feel uncomfortable with someone looking at her with leering eyes? That would have been rational. I couldn't help rebuking myself why had I ogled at her so embarrassingly.

That night I didn't feel like going to a nightclub again. Her large fair eyes were my constant afterimage. I couldn't sleep for longer than half an hour. My penis got hard then and again. My heart raced only for the thought of those shaved long legs and that slim feminine build which showcased the perfect curves of an attractive young woman. A young woman who had to be adored, had to be worshiped. I imagined her lying beside me, there, in my tiny student bed. Each and every time

29

in that repeated reverie, her charm and aroma forced me in one direction: downwards. I stripped her of all her clothes, bra and panties. She'd have a thong ebony one. And my tongue slowly stroked her skin and savored its salty flavor and slid past her navel and further down. There in my dream, her hand was dominant, and she knew exactly what she wanted and where my mouth was destined to land. Her labia were juicy and soft, and her moaning a music to my ears.

Ω Ω Ω

"So what do you study?"

It was a very simple question. I told you I was studying Organic Chemistry and I should have answered that question quick as a bunny, but I was speechless. I couldn't believe Sandra had accepted to drink coffee with me in the university café. "Chemistry," I stammered after a moment of pause, "and you?" I think I must have seemed way odd to her with the way I faltered.

"Psychology!" her voice was soft and her eyes curious and smart.

"Psychology must be very interesting!"

"Oh yeah?! So you don't know any other line to attract a woman?"

I wondered. What did she mean?!

"Excuse me! I don't get?!"

"Nothing, it's just it's getting boring. No matter who invites me to a coffee, my first conversation follows a repeated pattern. The second sentence is always what you just said."

"Oh, I am sorry. But I mean it."

"So if you mean that then why are you studying chemistry?"

"I didn't think much about that actually."

"You didn't think much about what you were going to study at university and thus your job for the rest of your life?! What about do you think instead? Or you don't like thinking at all?!"

Soon my mind was in a muddle. I hadn't thought over my field of study as to why I had chosen it deeply back then but I was also not interested to talk about that in detail at that moment. However, Sandra was a stern and precise woman who wanted to meticulously scrutinize me. As if she was already planning her future with a potential candidate whose character must be examined carefully. It

30

actually surprised me a bit because we Germans are so liberal in relationships between men and women that most of the time we even are oblivious of the gender of our conversation partner or the person with who we share our coffee break. Therefore, I cheered in my heart that what we'd begun would not end in mere simple friendship but there was hope that we would be together in near future, of course if I'd pass the tests the gracious blond lady was to subject me to, and indeed many came to be quite trying.

Well that comes over you if you date a psychologist, or in this case a psychology student. In our coffee breaks I found out that the vast majority of the psychology students at university were women, so that had been the source of my great luck. She had definitely thought of me as a boyfriend candidate because of the male gender being scarce in her environment.

Ω Ω Ω

The weather was getting warmer as summer had arrived in the temperate regions of the Northern Hemisphere. Female students of our university had discarded their warmers and long skirts to wear short ones which barely covered their groins or hot pants short of concealing their thighbrows. Those thighbrows! I love to watch them on women. My heart beats fast whenever I look at them from behind, especially if their owner has laid the palms of her hands on her waist and has parted her legs to a distance from each other. It conveys an air of pride, and you could revel in the view of a tough lady. But I was not keeping watch on no lady that day, because I was accompanying and chatting with the ANGEL of my life, although we were still only friends.

We strolled down a walkway running past the library with its huge glass structure, past the faculty of Chemistry and Physical Chemistry, and leading to a pond at the end of its buildings which in spring and summer brimmed with ever croaking frogs. On the side of the path opposite the faculty it was green with lots of trees, some of which were relatively large apple and pear ones. There were other walkways crossing the main walkway in almost right angles, and they ran through the greenery and seemingly into the forest behind it, so we had abundant room to promenade. It was there when our intimacy finally scintillated.

I think we were already near that pond with the mentioned croaking frogs that Sandra decided to sit down on a bench. Instead of sitting myself on it too, I squatted on the ground in front of her, my head near her knees and bare flesh. She was comfortable enough not to object. I looked at her and laughed without a reason, like a fool. I lost my balance and my face landed between her thighs. I grabbed her knees and pulled myself out of that wonderful, however embarrassing situation. She didn't move. I knew in a trice that was the opportunity. I took hold of her hand and kissed it. She kept looking at me without any especial reaction. I kissed it again. "You like me, don't you?" Her voice was soft.

"More than everything! I will kiss your feet if you'd let me!"

"Really! I like that."

I moved for her foot but she pushed me back, "Are you crazy?! Here is university!"

"But there's no one around!"

"You stupid dumbass! What if someone sees us? And I didn't say that you are allowed to do that! We are only friends!"

"Maybe that could be the beginning of something new!"

"No it can't. Not like this! Have you ever tried to win a woman's heart?! You don't do it with offering to kiss her feet! That's disgusting!"

"But you said you like it!"

"That's exactly what I mean! You're just stupid. You just speak your mind without thinking. You don't have to say directly what you want. You should have a plan. You must be smart."

She stood up, still looking vexed. "Ok I will leave now, I have a lecture, and I won't come back to the library this afternoon."

I was dumbfounded. I didn't know what she had talked about. She'd said that she liked that I kissed her foot but that at the same time it was disgusting, and I was stupid.

$$\Omega \quad \Omega \quad \Omega$$

That other day I sat there again at that desk. I hadn't seen Sandra for a week now. She hadn't replied my messages. How hard life was without her. Should I go that evening to the club again? I really didn't feel like going there to meet a stranger. I heaved a deep sigh and opened my book. I tried to get absorbed in it for time to pass faster. "Hi Armin," Sandra's voice started me after only five minutes.

I turned around and she stood there again, with a really short skirt and black tank top having a very low neckline which showed off half of her breasts. Didn't I tell you we Germans are liberal? That's how many girls had turned up at the university's library that day. I swallowed my breath. I was on cloud nine! "Sandra!"

32

"Do you have time for a coffee?"

"Sure!"

At coffee I was scared stiff. Was she there to rebuke me for my uncommon behavior and to end our friendship?

"So you don't want to say anything?" She sounded calm and serene as always.

"Yes, I am sorry for being silent. So how are you? Where were you all last week?"

"I preferred to study at home. Here in the library it is often loud, so I can't concentrate so well!"

"So you're not coming any longer?"

"Well today I am here... I missed you."

My heart was going to explode. I shook, so happy I was. "I missed you too."

"So you like to kiss my foot?"

That knocked my socks off. I got a hard on at once. "More than everything." I was shivering.

"Where do you live?"

"Schiller street."

"Oh that's a bit far from where I live. But it's ok."

"Should we go now?"

She laughed, "No you fool, I have come here to study. You must wait for the evening."

Ω Ω Ω

It was strange. Women are different from men, or was Sandra different from all humans? She got engrossed in her books with a focused look on her eyes, but that day I couldn't focus on reading at all. I kept staring at her. She noticed that, but didn't make a remark.

Ω Ω Ω

When we arrived in my dormitory room, Sandra gave vent to a groan of sorrow, "Oh, your room is so tiny! It's diminutive! How can you live here?" She said while sitting herself on my bed. I had one room of only 7 square meters with everything inside, my bed, my desk and my washbasin. Of course the bathroom was shared among the rooms.

"I don't know," I said as my voice shivered. She put her handbag to a corner and sat on the bed. She fixed me with her gaze. I kneeled on the floor in front of her. I couldn't wait any longer.

"You may."

"I may?!"

"Yes, you may," her tone was haughty.

I took hold of her foot. She still had her white sneaker on. I didn't dare take it off. I just slowly raised it to my face and kissed its tip, and then its sole. I could hear Sandra breathing heavily. Finally I had succeeded to impress her, to move her. "You can take it off!" Her voice was soft this time.

I was so chilly I had to hug myself once. I trembled wildly. I was happy Sandra was kind enough not to laugh at me. I was happy I managed to take that shoe off without having a heart attack. I sucked on her toes covered in her sock. "Take the sock off! Armin, don't kiss my sock it's disgusting. Take it off!" Her tone was aggressive. I obeyed and striped her foot of that pink sock. I kissed those feet which had the color of marble. It smelled a bit. I was surprised. Was Sandra not an angel? When I think back to my emotions at those moments I laugh at how foolish I was, how much in love. Of course her foot would smell after one whole day in a shoe. A lover never rejects anything their sweetheart has to offer, a lover worships it. I grew to like her smell. I kept busy kissing and licking and sucking her toes. "Take them off" My heart was pounding. Was it real? Had she just asked me to take her panties off? I obeyed my love's order. I reached for her sexy string panties and pulled them off. Her labia appeared. She was shaved and her pink slit peeked out from between them as if summoning to take pleasing action right away. I pushed her legs a bit farther apart from each other, and slowly approached my face to her buttocks. I was still hesitant, I kissed her crotch and licked my lips to test her taste. It was a bit sour. She also smelled of sweet. I don't say I was keen on eating out not exactly a clean pussy, but the view, those fleshy buttocks and those slender long legs, her feet which she'd laid now on my head and drove me into a downright sweet humiliation, the view of her nipples jutting out from beside her bra as she rubbed them playfully, all left me no other choice. I licked her labia for long. In the end she moaned loud. She enfolded my head in her thighs, shaking, until she calmed down. She sat up again and pushed me back with her foot. She

34

didn't ask me if I needed gratification too. It seemed I still didn't earn her care. I had to work hard to persuade her to let me put my dick into her: kissing, licking and caressing her. When I did put my dick inside her, it was going to explode right at the beginning, but I went all out not to come. A few minutes later, we were shaking while we held ourselves in each other's tight embraces.

Ω Ω Ω

When we both calmed down Sandra caressed my hair affectionately as I lay on her in her arms. She'd revealed the passionate side of her soul to me. I never forget the gaze of those unbelievably comely eyes. I never let go of the memories of those amazing moments.

Ω Ω Ω

I couldn't believe Sandra wanted to introduce me to her mother. Her father had divorced his wife when Sandra had been only ten years old and considering that she had no siblings, her mother was all what meant family to her. I was nervous and excited. I hoped her mother wouldn't react badly at the first moment. I'd had bad memories of women treating me disparagingly, mothers at whose homes I tutored their children.

Ω Ω Ω

I want to be honest with you, I had never thought tutelage would be such a pain in my ass. The most difficult time was when I called at the family after having made the arrangements via phone call. The mother would say, "Oh, are you sure you're a university student?! You look too young to be one. Your voice sounded so mature over the phone!" I always hated people being judgmental about me, and what is more judgmental than people thinking you're still a teenager although you are almost 24?! Funny enough, that roughness right at the beginning made me more or less softer than what I usually was, forcing smiles at moments they handled me like I'd just fallen off the turnip truck, the moments they refused to pay me as agreed for delusional reasons such as I hadn't been hardworking enough when teaching their lazy child. One or two times those haughty women were so aggressive that I implicitly offered them, of course after a long chat over the mobile's SMS, to eat them out to be paid properly in return. Well they did accept that offer, but refuted any relation between being served with a young agilely wiggling tongue in their pussy and the necessity to compensate the owner of that entertaining tongue with a due sum. Those days we still didn't know the likes of WhatsApp. Actually as I foresaw altercations as to my remuneration quite at the beginning of my every tutorage, I very soon asked the mother for a phone number to begin softening her heart parallel to my endeavors centered on teaching her child.

35

A conversation over SMS would look at the beginning of the teaching period like this:

-"Hello Mrs. Müller, I wanted to thank you for the delicious cup of coffee you served last night. It tasted really good."

-"Hi Armin! You're welcome. But you didn't try the cookies."

-"Oh I did. They were yummy too. I feel very well when I am at your home, thanks for the hospitality."

-"You're very welcome! I'm glad you liked them. You are very kind, Armin, thank you!"

-"So goodnight Mrs. Müller"

And then I finished the SMS with the emoji of a rose flower. It worked very well, most of the time, as a beginning. In the case of Mrs. Müller she rose to the bait at once. She sent a huge kiss, unknowing that she was trapped in a sophisticated game in whose end she was shivering naked on the same sofa where I had tried her cookies the first time, her legs wide apart as I licked and sucked her labia with still more appetite than I had shown for her dainty cookies. That time I even went shortly for her anus, only a short kiss, and she exploded in joy. I have drawn a rule out of that. Women who enjoy a mouth around their sphincter are aggressive and self-confident, assertive enough to become successful and climb up fast the carrier ladder. In her case, she was the manager of a small company, seldom in Germany. Well, she too, had forgotten that I had swallowed every drop of her squirt that other night. She paid me around 50 euros less than what we'd originally agreed. Still I held back any objection, there was a chance I would be offered another tutorage with the hostess bearing in mind the prospect that she would receive a magnificent cunnilingus from me again.

Ω Ω Ω

Anyway when Sandra's mother opened the door to their luxurious apartment in one of the most expensive districts of Düsseldorf I was flabbergasted for a long moment. She was a copy of her daughter. Sandra, had she been a bit taller and much older, around late forties, would look exactly like her mother. Folk wisdom has it that everyone has a doppelganger, so the resemblance between a mother and her own child shouldn't be surprising. But I think it was not that similarity that almost made my heart jump out of my chest, but the very fact that I was in love with that face, body and shape, and now I met it in a slightly different quality, somehow like a nuance of something adorable, and certainly a pleasant one, and there lay the conundrum: I was deeply in love with Sandra. I sometimes didn't drink water for hours after eating her out only not to let go of the taste of her pussy in my mouth. Yes, love can be sweet and painful at the very same time, forcing you to put up with thirst for hours. Yet now I saw her mature copy, and I fall so easily for mature beauties.

Anja (we Germans read this Anya) had a black leather jacket and a skirt which reached almost up to above her knees. She didn't have glasses like her daughter, and the beauty emanated from those green eyes would put every discerning observer under a spell. She gave a huge smile which dissolved the fear in my heart in an instant.

Anja invited us into their apartment and ushered me into a modern looking living room. A rectangular glass table stood in the middle with several metal chairs around. There was a magazine rack in one corner and another rack abutted the wall beside it with lots of wine and gin bottles. The decoration seemed amusing to me. "Please, feel yourself at home. Please take a seat." Anja's voice was kind and hospitable. We both sat at the table like two good kids after Sandra pointed to the seat where I supposed to sit, as always showing me the way. Anja remained on her feet and asked what we'd like to drink. "I would savor a cup of coffee, Mrs. Schelleder."

At this moment Sandra glared at me, "Armin you are not supposed to drink coffee now! You told me you cannot sleep well in the night if you drink coffee late in the evening."

"But I do like one."

"No you don't." Sandra's stance was clear and I gave up, although it saddened me that she treated me somewhat humiliating right at the first time I met her mother. Anja didn't contradict her daughter. Apparently her hospitality had vivid boundaries, but her smile remained, "So what do you like to drink then, chai?"

"What is chai?!"

"Indian black tea."

"Oh yes please, if I'm not allowed to drink coffee, then my second choice would be a glass of tea." I know I am a sissy, this was the farthest I could go to voice my objection, if I even did so.

"Great! Do you also fancy some cookies? I have baked them myself."

This last sentence made my spine hair stand on end. I suddenly thought of Mrs. Müller. "Sure," I said, and then thought of that SMS I had sent to Mrs. Müller to set the ball rolling with a chain reaction which ended in my head stuck between her white shaved fleshy thighs and my tongue swirling around her pink slit. Some idea dawned on me, but I tried to concentrate on the present moment and savor the cup of chai and cookies Mrs. Schelleder had baked herself. She had sat on the chair opposite me, but I could see how she put one leg on the other and I could see her black panties through the glass table under her red skirt.

"Sandra says you are quite a hardworking student!"

I doubted that Sandra had mentioned my tirelessness to her mother, but while gulping down a bunch of those tasty cookies, I replied, "Oh thank you! I am delighted to hear that."

I noticed a mocking smile on Sandra's lips, but I ignored and got busy with drinking and eating.

After our visit, Sandra accompanied me on the way back home to downtown. It was a clear night and a balmy breeze invigorated the soul. We took the way along the bank of Rhine River. The Düsseldorf TV-tower towered over the city with an amazing impression. The moon was almost full and you could see its reflection on Rhine's surface. I was absorbed in thoughts. May God forgive me, I couldn't help but think of Sandra's mother. I felt so ashamed that it depressed me. I loved Sandra more than everything and I felt being so depraved that I couldn't eject her mother's comely face out of my mind's eye. I remembered what my grandmother once told me, that most men are cranks. I let out a sigh and Sandra got notice, "What's the matter dear?"

"Nothing, just the moon affects my mood."

"Does it make you sad?"

"No, not at all," I forced a chuckle.

"I think my mother really likes you."

"You think so?!"

"Sure. I know her. I could see it in her sparkling eyes."

"Sparkling?! I didn't notice anything."

"Yes, you weren't looking at her that much. Because you have only eyes for me," she winked and smiled.

"I just thought she was very kind and hospitable."

Ω Ω Ω

That night Sandra poured us a lot of French white wine. I didn't have any champagne at home, so we'd resorted to white wine instead. We wanted to celebrate our first step in our relationship, that she had introduced me to her mother. I think we both knew it was only an excuse to get drunk and enjoy ourselves. She made sure that I drink more, so she could take control as always. I think I emptied two bottles, more than enough to intoxicate me. Later in bed, she restrained my wrists to the grates of my headbed with her two socks, and undressed herself as she stood over my head. She gazed in my eyes as she slowly squatted on my face, and my lips touched her privates. Soon there was no room for me to react or move any longer. She firmly grasped my head and rubbed her vulva hard on my face. I couldn't see much in the dark, except for the fleshy buttocks of my girlfriend. Her juices ran down on my face and into my mouth. Wasn't it beautiful that I had the chance?! A graceful and smart woman offering me her womanly juices for free? But of a sudden, I thought of her mother. How would she taste? Again I felt remorseful. Sandra was moaning loud, unaware of my perfidious thoughts.

Ω Ω Ω

Later that night, I promised myself I won't think of her mother again. Someday Sandra would look as gorgeous and mature as her mother looked. I looked forward to that day.

Ω Ω Ω

"Hello Mrs. Schelleder. I just wanted to thank you for your kind hospitality the other night."

"Excuse me! Who's there? I don't have your number in my contacts."

"This is me, Armin Zeitler, your daughter's boyfriend."

"Oh gosh Armin! Dear Armin! You just frightened me a bit. How are you?"

"Thank you! I am fine. Sandra has gone to the university already."

"Oh, I just wanted to send my greetings to my daughter. I sometimes miss her but children grow and leave their parents' home, that's life."

"I'm sorry to have taken Sandra away from you."

"You are sweet! That's life. She's not a child any longer."

"I love her. She looks beautiful. She is the hottest woman I've ever met."

39

"That's a good sign! It means you're in love. I am happy for you both."

"You look so much like her, and you're beautiful too!"

"Yes I know. Thanks for the compliment. Anyway she's my daughter. That shouldn't surprise you. But now I am old and not that beautiful as I used to be, and as she is now."

"Actually I find older women sexier."

Mrs. Schelleder didn't reply.

Ω Ω Ω

No need to say I didn't keep my promise to myself. I had deliberated a lot as to try to seduce Mrs. Schelleder to some kind of flirting. Only flirting I swear. I found her so hot I could masturbate only if I could playfully adore her with words and she would listen. But it had apparently gone amiss. She didn't reply to me when I had written that I found older women sexier.

The next evening I had arrived home earlier than Sandra. I was scared. What if Anja had told her about what I had written her? Suddenly, my mobile vibrated. It was a message from Sandra. My heart missed a beat. I opened the message quick.

"Hey Armin! I will be arriving late tonight. I just met a colleague and we want to discuss a project we both have to do for one of our courses. We are in the same group. Would you do me a favor? I have forgotten to fetch my book of Social Psychology from my mum's. Could you go over to her and fetch it?"

I didn't dare go there, so I made up an excuse, "Sandra, I'm sorry. I have a headache."

"Really? Ok. Don't worry. I will tell mum to bring that book over."

"Oh no, here is such a mess. Don't do that."

"It'll be ok, I will tell her not to come in."

"No Sandra, listen! I will go there myself."

"Are you sure?! I thought you had a headache."

"I have taken some medicine. I'll be fine soon."

I was a little perplexed. It seemed there was no relationship with no problems involved. It reminded me of the women I had met in discotheques and their nagging at whatever relationship they'd been in. I just dressed up and left. I was afraid how Anja would react to seeing me again.

When I arrived, it took a while till I dared to ring the bell. She picked up the door entry phone. "Hello"

"Hello Mrs. Schelleder, I am here to..."

"Hi Armin," her voice was kind! "Yes, Sandra told me about the book. Come on up."

She remotely opened the entrance door to the building and I was shortly upstairs at the apartment door which was already open a crack. I entered the apartment calling out, "Hello! Mrs. Schelleder"

She appeared from the kitchen with a big smile and wearing very short shorts. "Hello Armin, sorry that I look like this, I didn't have time to sort myself out."

I wondered if she'd dressed like that deliberately. Maybe she liked me and wanted to show me bare skin as far as she could? Now that I think back to that I am sure she did not. Her hair looked disheveled and her face unwashed. She had probably been sleeping, and wasn't expecting me, although Sandra had told her that I was calling. However, in that moment, with my juvenile thoughts I took it for a try to attract me. It was wrong, but often in life, wrong assumptions may cause you to take the risk and come out ahead. That gesture melted all of my tension away, and goaded me to ogle at her body noticeably as she stood in front of me. She noticed the direction of my eyes but it didn't seem to bother her. Was it because I looked younger than my age and like so many other women she didn't take me seriously? Or maybe she didn't take my relationship with her daughter not so earnest? "You could go to her room and fetch the book yourself if you want."

"Sure Mrs. Schelleder."

She chuckled, "Please call me Anja, Mrs Schelleder sounds very awkward."

I went into Sandra's room which was just around the corner from the living room. It was five times larger than my dormitory room. She had a king size bed and two huge wardrobes on the side of the room opposite the large windows which looked over the lush park in the vicinity of the house. On the side opposite the door she had a desk with drawers. I was not sure if I was allowed to look into them, but I couldn't see the book on the desk. There were a couple of Spanish course books instead. I opened the first drawer and it was full of markers, sticky tapes and other stationery. I tried to open the second drawer. I have to laugh when I think of that moment. I couldn't open it because I hadn't completely pushed back in the first one. Many drawer racks are like that. I didn't come up with the solution.

I was confused as I saw no lock hole on it. I tried the third drawer but had the same problem. "Armin is everything all right?! Did you find the book?" Anja called out to me after a while as I was tinkering with the drawers. "Sorry Mrs. Schelleder, but I can't open up the drawers!" My answer was embarrassingly, maybe stupidly honest. Anja appeared faster than what I had expected. "You call me Mrs. Schelleder again. You don't like to call me by first name?"

"Oh I'm sorry I didn't mean to. No, it's fine Anja, it was just a blunder."

"Push the first completely in," I saw a subtle smile on her face but still couldn't make out what she was saying.

"Push the first?"

She came over to the desk and shoved the first drawer in with a punch.

"Oh I see!"

She drew the second open and there was the book. She handed it to me. I wondered why she still wore those 'very short' shorts. Besides, her décolleté was so low I could see most of her bosom. Her nipples were visible either. I stared at them boldly saying, "Anja sorry for that message that day."

"No problem Armin, I am not that huffy," and then she floored me, "you like older women, don't you? You can't keep your eyes off me?!"

How much I wanted to ask her if I could go down on her, but again Sandra's pretty face flashed before my eyes and I held back. I remained silent. I am happy I didn't. Suffering the repentance would have been a downright devastating tribulation.

Ω Ω Ω

I noticed that the sun was setting and its rays were kindling the sky with oranges and reds. Anja followed the direction of my view and saw that too. We stood up together and went to the window. It was beautiful. The green of the park and the Rhine and the skyline of Düsseldorf all together had outlined a breathtaking view. I reached for Anja's hand and squeezed it firmly in my hand. "I thank you Anja. Thank you for bringing an angel into the world."

She didn't say anything. She pressed my hand hard.

The Girl on the Train

Having finished my studies at the University of Düsseldorf, I had to search several months till I found a job. It was in Duisburg, a city northwards from Düsseldorf. Duisburg has a population of around 500,000. It's smaller than Düsseldorf, as Düsseldorf has around one million inhabitants. However, it's never as beautiful. I'd been living in Düsseldorf for 20 years now. I loved this city. It was lovely to visit. It has magnificent and beautiful streets, where lots of nice and lustrous shops glim.

Having got the job, another problem arose. It was extremely difficult to find an apartment in Duisburg. The apartments were either too expensive, or they were located in the outskirts. Finally I was lucky enough to find a reasonably priced apartment near Duisburg's clinic, not far from the city center. It was quite a large one for the price, considering the current high prices everywhere in Germany—50 square meters for a rent of around €800. I had a modern, fully furnished kitchen with a dishwasher, and two sets of furniture in the living room, plus a very small, however convenient sleeping room.

Although being finally settled in Duisburg, the beauty of Düsseldorf was a constant attraction to me. I decided to keep the apartment I had in Düsseldorf and continue to pay the rent, in spite of it being quite a burden. In this way I could come from time to time to Düsseldorf to meet with my many years-long friends.

It took the train around two hours to reach Duisburg from Düsseldorf or the other way round. I took the *Agilis* trains, which are a type of German Regional Railways (in German: *Regional Bahn*). These are quite nice and clean, compared to other Regional trains. I commuted two times per week. Once on Monday morning from Düsseldorf to Duisburg, having spent the weekend in Düsseldorf, and again I returned back to Düsseldorf directly after work on Friday afternoon.

Travelling over this stretch was not boring at all, as it was two times per week in all. Besides, I used the time to read books I had wanted to read for so long. Thanks to modern technology, and my new Kindle device, a gift from my sister, at least I didn't have to carry huge books around, relieving the burden a bit.

One day, while reclining back on a seat in the train, resting my feet on the opposite seat, almost curling up, and as I was absorbed in reading that wordy book, suddenly the gentle voice of a woman brought me back to reality:

"Hey, Armin! Is that you?!"

I looked up to the woman standing beside my seat. It took me a while till her face rang a bell. She looked older than she'd used to ten years before, but at last I could recognize her, it was Manuela!

"May I sit here?" she asked.

I brightened up. "Of course," I said, "How are you?"

"Fine!" She said while she was taking a seat, "what are you doing here?" she asked with a big smile.

"I'm going back to Düsseldorf. I'm coming from Duisburg at the moment."

"Why?"

"I'm working there, at *Teknelek*, we produce spare parts for cars."

"Oh, interesting!" she replied.

"And you?" I asked, looking out through the window to realize in which train station we'd just been to figure out where she'd got on, as I'd been completely absorbed in my history book up to that moment, "is here *Donauwörth*?"

"Yes"

"And what are you doing here? Are you working here?"

"Yes, I am working at *Erko*," she replied.

"Erko?"

"Yes, they produce control systems for helicopters…"

I cut her off, "for arms industry?" I asked.

She looked a little bit annoyed, "Yes, is that a problem?" she asked.

"No, everybody should decide for themselves. I think it should be very interesting, at least much more interesting than what I'm doing. So are you working as an electrical engineer?"

"Yes, like you. You remember?"

"Yes, anyway it's been a long while since we met last time, ten years I guess?"

"Yes, it's unbelievable, isn't it? Ten damn years!" she replied.

$$\Diamond \quad \Diamond \quad \Diamond$$

"Ten damn years!" I replied.

I thought back to when we two had met for the first time. Daniel, my classmate from Columbia, had introduced us to each other. We set off for *Oktoberfest* that day, the world's largest *Volksfest*, a combination of a huge beer festival and a travelling funfair, held annually in Munich. The trains driving from Düsseldorf to Munich were completely full, we were lucky to catch one but we had to stand during the whole trip, which lasted more than four hours, with that Regional Railways train. I and Manuela talked a lot during the journey, as Daniel, although having the same mother tongue as Manuela, namely Spanish, remained mostly silent as he's a bit coy. We talked about many different topics. Manuela is a very interesting person. She's very intelligent. Although she comes from a small village somewhere in the south of Spain, and despite having been quite young back then, around 20 years old, as old as I was, she'd had a lot of experience in her life hitherto.

We met a lot of people on the fest, and funnily many thought that we two were siblings. I never knew that two strangers could look so similar.

We met several boys, I think from Italy, as they had quite a dark complexion. They wanted to kiss Manuela right away, and she constantly eluded the insisting boys with different excuses.

We drank a lot of beer, and danced in one of the huge beer tents. At some point, Manuela looked quite intoxicated. Suddenly, a good-looking boy appeared out of the blue, also an Italian I guess. Italians are experts in attracting women. He asked her if they could dance. I could see the sparkle of lust and bliss in Manuela's beautiful eyes. After dancing for only two minutes, they kissed!

It was very funny! Daniel seemed very pissed off. "European girls are bitches!" he said. I realized in that moment that Daniel had grown feelings for Manuela, and that he was very jealous of that allegedly Italian boy.

But I felt happy for her. She looked very content. On the trip back we found seats to sit on. Manuela was sitting beside me. The lots of alcohol had rendered her dazed. She felt some cramp in her back. I offered to massage her. "Yes," she said.

As I was massaging her beautiful, slim body, Manuela was moaning at one moment. It was apparently very pleasant for her. She turned around momentarily and said, "Kiss me Armin!"

"No!" I replied.

"Why? You don't like me?"

"You don't know what you're saying now. You're drunk. Just try to keep calm."

Instead I reached for her hand and kissed it. She smiled.

"I kissed you now," I said with a smile.

She moved closer to me, and put her head on my chest. I caressed her beautiful curly hair.

"Try to sleep, Spanish princess," I whispered in her ear, as I continued fondling her soft hair.

◊　　◊　　◊

Suddenly a loud announcement in German bellowing over the speaker brought me back to my senses.

"Next Stop, *Günzburg*!"

Manuela said, "You were pondering."

"Oh, I was thinking about the work."

"I feel tired, today I got on the train at 6:30 in the morning," she said.

"You commute there each day?"

"Yes, it's a catastrophe, it's so exhausting. And the job is so stressful. If you don't mind, I would stretch out my legs and put my feet on the seat beside you."

"No, not at all!" I replied.

Manuela fell asleep soon, covering herself with her pink overcoat. I also continued with my book. I began with the place where Empress Maria was appointed as the Queen of the Byzantine Empire, and Babylonians were attacking the Empire's border to the east.

However, after a while, I felt sleepy too. I put the Kindle Reader to a side. I looked at Manuela, she looked so sweet while sleeping. She had such a maiden innocence on her face. Her beautiful sable hair cascading down, past her shoulders. While glaring at this pretty creature, I lost myself in the fantasies of the curls and ringlets of that lustrous, regal hair, of those regular, attractive lineaments, and that shapely, slim body. I asked myself, "Was Empress Mari also so attractive?"

While watching and enjoying this magnificent and comely sight, and while absorbed in my thoughts, I fell asleep.

◊   ◊   ◊

I was riding on a gilded gelding. To my left, a Roman knight was carrying the insignia of the Byzantine Empire. We had just crushed an army of Babylonian militants, and had routed them.

At the gate of the White Castle in Constantinople, two lines of soldiers were standing on the stairs to the main entrance. As soon as we arrived they blew into their horns to welcome me and my troops. Yes, in my dream I was the commander of the Roman army.

People were cheering us, and throwing flowers at us. The Grand Minister came down the stairs. "Well done! General Augustus!" He said. Now I also knew my name in my dream.

He guided me into the castle. It was unbelievable. I hadn't seen something as beautiful hitherto. The gilded furniture, and the in reddish and cyan stained window glasses bestowed a glorious air to the castle.

"We've all been praying for many days for your glorious victory," the Grand Minister said while walking me to the main hall.

"With your help and the help of Jesus Christ, we prevailed at last, we crushed the Babylonians!" I said.

"God Almighty never helps people who don't help themselves, you should be proud of yourself, General!" The Grand Minister said.

We entered the main hall. A very large Persian rug was covering the floor. It had a green background and was decorated with lustrous, pink and yellow flowers, and images of attractive women with breasts uncovered. Pictures of colossal mountains were ornamenting the walls.

In the middle of the hall, Empress Maria awaited me. She was looking through the window upon the Garden of Roses. She was wearing a gilded, inlaid crown. Although I hadn't seen Maria t up to that time, I recognized that curly, sable hair.

The Empress turned around and showed off her beautiful, regal face. She smiled at me affectedly while walking toward me, and reached her hand out for me. I grabbed that delicate hand and kissed it. I looked up to the Empress again. Now, from nearby, I could see her face better. I could not believe. It was Manuela!

"Manuela?! Is that you?" I asked surprisedly, "what are you doing here?"

The Empress bestowed an affected look upon me and smirked.

"Are you out of your mind General Augustus?!" She said.

"No! Manuela, you don't remember me?! We were sitting on the train, I think around half one hour ago."

The Empress cut in, "What is an hour? What is a train?" She replied, "I think the battle has rattled you. You need to take a rest. Nevertheless, I congratulate you upon the defeat you inflicted on the Babylonians."

At that moment, the Empress waved the Grand Minister to leave the room and to close the large double door behind him.

Then, the Empress, I mean Manuela or now apparently Empress Maria, entwined me in her warm embrace. She had the fragrance of White Roses. It was so pleasant! But she suddenly pressed upon my head, forcing me downwards. I was confused, and I resisted.

"What are you doing Manuela?" I asked.

"Go down," she replied, "and if you call me with this strange name again I will order that they cut your tongue out of your mouth. I am the regent here. You are the army commander, but I am still the Queen. You must obey me with your heart and soul."

"What do you mean? Go down where?"

"On me," she replied.

"No!" I said again.

Suddenly she slapped my face, and she pushed me down again, while saying "Augustus, don't say you've forgotten that you love me. You liked it so much before you left two weeks ago. You know that we can't sleep together before we marry, and that we can't marry because of the current politics and the state of the country. So this is the only way you can serve my pleasure…"

This time I did not resist, I found that everything that was happening made sense in this new, alien universe. She led me down, holding a tight grip on my head, showing that she was a deserving reign, dominant and assertive. I was reluctant to give her head at first. I touched her with my puckered up lips, and then tasted her a little. She tasted salty, but pleasant. I tried again, and again. Shortly after, I lost myself in the bliss of eating out her royal body. As I was floating in the universe of dreams, and as I was tasting the most wonderful flavors, suddenly and sadly I heard a disruptive noise reverberating in my cozy, snug position under Empress Maria's hoop skirt, between her thighs. It said, in harsh German, "*Nächste Haltestelle, Donauwörth Hauptbahnhof. Bitte steigen Sie links aus,*" meaning, "Next stop Donauwörth central station. Please exit the train on the left." I realized with a wrenched heart that I had to leave that beautiful world, the next moment I found myself reclining on the train's seat, opposite to Manuela, who was looking at me with her beautiful light-colored eyes.

Having left the universe of dreams in agony, she bestowed a warm, charming smile on me. I felt happy and hopeful again, as I saw Manuela, or Empress Maria directly in front of my eyes straightaway. With her sweet way of speaking German with Spanish accent, blending the contrasts of these two incongruous languages, she said, "you looked so sweet while you were sleeping." This one sentence cheered my heart up and it began to beat fast. I hope this was not reflected in my face, as it would have been very embarrassing. I said, "thank you! You are so kind to me, princess!" I really don't know why I said princess in my rejoinder. Did I want to flirt with her, unwittingly, or was I mixing her up with the woman I had gone down on moments before in my dream? Anyway, Manuela laughed and said, "Wow, you remind me of that Italian guy I met once in Oktoberfest. I think you were also there. Do you remember? Many years ago."

"Why?" I answered.

"You know, he called me a princess and asked to kiss me a few moments later," she said.

"I remember you two kissed. I remember you looked very happy with that. Your eyes were shining with affection."

"Oh, but it was not that serious, I mean, what you saw in my eyes," she said, "after all, I'd been boozing the entire day, I was quite intoxicated."

"But what's the difference? Being drunk doesn't make a difference. We're always drunk, if not out of alcohol, we're drunk because of something else. Being

49

in love perfectly resembles being drunk. One loses their mind and follows their heart."

"Ok, maybe you're right, but believe me, nothing happened between the two of us afterwards. He called me only once, and never again," she said.

"Yes, it's none of my business anyway," I said.

"But did you manage to find your way home that night? You looked very confused," she asked.

"Oh I did. I'd filled myself with lots of beer, but I managed it."

"Ok Armin, that was nice to see you again after these many years. Take care, we will see each other again, here," she said.

"Definitely, however I commute over to Duisburg only every Monday, as I said. So we will see each other on next Monday."

"Or on Friday, when you'll go back from Duisburg to Düsseldorf," Manuela replied.

"Yes! See you on Friday then! Have a nice day!"

"Same to you! Good bye," she said.

◊   ◊   ◊

I didn't see Manuela on Friday. On Monday, as I was lounging on my seat, she walked past my seat, but she looked very tired, no wonder as it was half past six in the morning. I didn't dare to approach her as I assumed it would be disturbing to force her into talking while she would certainly prefer to rest. She walked to the front of the train and reclined back on the seat there. She covered herself with her overcoat and slowly shut her beautiful eyes.

◊   ◊   ◊

Weeks passed by and every Monday morning I observed how Manuela walked past my seat only to end up at the front of the train to loll, or to sleep. But I didn't dare to nudge her while she was passing by, in order to offer her a seat and to talk to. I wasn't sure if she would like it. Anyway, she should have known that I was there on the same train on Monday morning. If she wanted to talk to me she should have paid some more attention to the seats, shouldn't she? Or had she forgotten me altogether?

Some people say our lots lie completely in our hands. I don't believe in this. In my life, luck has played in many cases a far bigger role in my fortunes than my own decisions and deeds.

I forewent her company completely, but one day the hand of fate tried to put our story on another track. While sitting on that train and turning the pages of a book on my Kindle Reader, all of a sudden, a hand tapped me on my shoulder gently.

"Hi Armin," said the delicate voice of a woman. I looked up to her only to see Manuela again, seeming tired, but delighted. "Can I sit beside you?" she asked.

"Sure!" I answered while collecting my bag, overcoat, gloves and cap from the seat beside me, making place for her to sit. "How are you?" I asked while watching her smiling face as she was hanging her overcoat on the small hook on the side of the window. "Fine," she answered with a warm tone. "I haven't seen you for around a month now I guess. Where have you been?" she continued.

"Well, I think you have probably forgotten. I take this train only once per week from Düsseldorf to Duisburg," I answered.

"Oh yes, I'm sorry…"

I cut her off to continue, "Actually I have been seeing you every Monday morning. However, I didn't want to disturb you so early. I have been watching how you went to the front of the train to take a nap each time."

She gave out a sweet smile and said, "Oh yes, you're right. It is very good to take a nap early in the morning. Otherwise the day would be so long!"

"I agree. Monday feels always a very long day for me. Each Monday morning I wonder if I can handle doing my job till five o'clock in the afternoon, until I leave work then," I said.

"Yes, you know, I have to return every day to Düsseldorf. It is very tedious," she said.

"Then I would not annoy you with keeping talking to you now. I can continue to read my e-book while you take a rest," I said.

51

"You're very kind Armin, so it would not be offensive to you if I take a nap here? If you don't mind I would like to stretch my legs onto the opposite seat," she said.

"No, not at all. Just take a rest," I replied.

"Ok," she said.

Manuela covered herself with her pink overcoat again and closed her blue, alluring eyes. As I watched this magnificent scene I saddened in my heart. I thought for a moment that how stupid I was to just let her sleep like that, to even propose that she should take a rest to have power for the upcoming day. I thought back about my other experiences with other women. I had keenly been longing to talk to her for around one month now. What a halfwit I was!

◊   ◊   ◊

As I was still pondering my lots, suddenly Manuela's voice brought me back to the present tense. "I am going Armin! It is Donauwörth, I will get off here." She was already standing beside the seat.

"Oh, ok. That's a pity we couldn't talk to each other this time," I replied.

She grinned baring her orderly, white teeth, "Next time, we will talk!" She said.

"Hopefully!" I answered.

◊   ◊   ◊

Several weeks had gone, till on one Friday, on the way back from Duisburg to Düsseldorf, in Donauwörth train station, Manuela got on the train, having seen me and having waved to me through the train's window. She seemed content and delighted, as she sat on the seat opposite to me. The Spanish are very good in talking. With her sweet, Spanish accent, Manuela started the conversation right away, "How are you? How is the job?"

"It's become quite boring actually, I am trapped in a vicious cycle. I am doing the same stuff every day. It is constantly repeating itself," I answered.

"The same with me, developing software can also be very tiring and tedious," she said, "the days are all the same."

Suddenly Manuela asked me a question which was the turning point of our story.

"Can you cook? It's a long time I haven't been to a restaurant." she said.

That was the huge opportunity. I had now an excuse to invite her home. "Of course," I said, "In Duisburg I have a large kitchen. You could visit me once, if you would like, and I will cook for you. I know some French dishes, and of course also German."

"I'm not sure when I have time, do you mean at the weekend or on a weekday?" She asked.

"Weekend would be more convenient for me, as during the week I am usually very tired in the evening having worked all day long," I answered.

"This weekend I can't, I will go to a wedding, but what about the next one?" She asked.

"It's perfect, give me your phone number so that I can add you on WhatsApp," I said.

"Ok, this is my number," she said before dictating it to me.

We continued talking as if nothing especial had happened, and certainly this held for Manuela. But for me, something wonderful had happened. My heart was beating faster than that of a small mouse. I was so happy! So happy!

◊   ◊   ◊

It was a wonderful Sunday. On Saturday, I had already bought all the necessary ingredients to cook a delicious Indian food whose recipe I had found on the internet, when the grocery stores had been open. I was cooking the so called *Rogan Josh*, a traditional Indian food made up of lamb meat, kidney beans, and herbs like parsley and coriander. I cooked some rice as the side dish, and ground some saffron in hot water and let it steep. I then spattered the resulting orange colored liquid on the rice, which looked yellow now. It scented great.

I was so cheerful! I was longing so much for the moment that Manuela would arrive. However, all of a sudden, sadness and sluggishness got the better of me. I thought for a moment, if all my excitement and cheer were for nothing, and that I could not touch Manuela that night. I began to become rational, and while continuing with cooking and then cleaning the apartment, I worked out a plan to persuade Manuela to let me give her head the same evening.

Manuela rang my bell at around 19:00 o'clock. She was nice enough to bring along a bottle of Spanish red wine, a bottle of *Marques de Caceres*, which I can spell out exactly as the bottle is still standing in the kitchen. While I guided her into my apartment, she was wearing that charming, heartwarming smile on her face, as usual. She liked my properly equipped, neat kitchen a lot. I think a kitchen is always a good thing to score with a woman. "Everything is new here, also the dishwasher, isn't it?" she said.

"Yes! But the equipment belongs to the apartment," I answered enthusiastically.

"How much are you paying for the rent?"

"Around €800 including the heating, and water," I answered.

"But that sounds ok in a city like Duisburg. I mean, considering that Audi Corporation has its headquarters and main factories here, the rents here must be generally quite high," she said.

"Yes, I was very lucky to find this."

I ushered her into the living room where my extremely comfortable one sofa and two armchairs stand. I tried to lead her to the sofa, with the intention to sit beside her later for the proximity, but before I could say anything she already sat herself in the armchair opposite to the TV. "This seat is very comfortable," she said.

"Yes, you're right," I said with a somewhat embarrassed tone.

"Can you turn on the TV please?" She asked.

I thought that the beginning of the evening had already slipped out of my control. As soon as I would turn on the TV, we would mind some program instead of ourselves. However, I couldn't refuse and turned it on. Worse was still to come, as some Spanish athletes were competing in some surfing competitions and Manuela insisted to watch that thing, instead of some romantic movie to which I was disposed to watch. Anyway, I returned to the kitchen and resigned myself to cooking.

Manuela didn't move from before the TV and I had to lay the table by myself. It felt a little odd, even somehow insulting, that she didn't offer to help me with anything. It disturbed my concentration even more. However, after a while, I felt better when she admired how good my dish smelt.

"It smells great," she said.

I brightened and said, "It's because of the herbs I've poured in, including parsley and coriander."

"But it can't be all that. It has some other scent inside. It is pleasant but I don't know it," she replied.

"You mean that of fenugreek?" I said.

"What? What did you just say?" She asked.

I smiled. I knew that few in Europe knew fenugreek. I repeated the German word for fenugreek, *Bockshornklee*, slowly for her. "In Germany they use it as an ingredient for some medicines," I added.

"I've never heard of that," she replied laughingly.

Her laughing relieved the anger of her not helping out, as I fetched everything necessary including two glasses, orange juice, wine, and yoghurt from the kitchen and set them out on the table.

The hard work paid off, Manuela looked happy and fascinated about how a man could arrange the cutlery, glasses, and the dishes so orderly. She fell in love with my *Rogan Josh* at the very first moment she put the first morsel in her mouth. It went on very well, and we talked and talked and talked. Her warm temperament, her beautiful eyes, and her cute Spanish accent were like a Sun warming my home.

At one moment, while the air had become very kind and cozy, I suddenly but deliberately descended from the sofa and sat on the floor beside her armchair. I tried to touch her hand and knees from time to time, as a means to build some bodily connection with her. It didn't seem to annoy her, but I also didn't dare to proceed any further. I thought I couldn't touch her thigh for example. It would be very odd. We continued talking heartily as I was losing my patience. My heart was burning with desire, and her elegance and sweetness was like a fan on that fire. I suddenly stood up and fetched a smaller chair from the other side of my room, as I couldn't move the huge sofa so easily, in order to sit closer to her. I wanted to play that old, known trick on her. I wanted to touch and stroke her hair and soften her heart so that she'd let me kiss her. But it didn't work! "What are you doing? Don't touch my hair!" She said looking a bit angry with me.

I felt ashamed and embarrassed. She was right! I had gone too far, too fast. An odd atmosphere pervaded in the room. Manuela looked not that kind anymore, but she also didn't stand up and go. I think she felt sorry for me, shortly after.

"Are you ok?" She said, "Look Armin, I didn't think you would see my visit as a date. I thought we are just friends."

"Yes, I know. I'm sorry. It was not planned. It was impulsive," I said but I knew exactly that I was lying.

Manuela smiled and said, "you like me, don't you?"

"A lot," I said.

"But the problem is that, I still don't know you right. This is too fast, too rash," she said.

I felt a sad chill in my heart. However, I pulled myself together and focused on what I was going to say again. While talking I mulled on different ways to persuade her to let me go down on her. However, I couldn't find any better sentence other than just telling her the truth and asking it from her frankly.

"So there is no way we could become more intimate tonight?" I asked again with a shivering voice, trying to look as sad and pathetic as I could to touch her heart and incite sorrow in her. I even managed to make watery eyes.

"No I'm sorry. Look, you're a nice guy, but this is too big a surprise. You're rushing me into something I'm not prepared for," she replied.

I remained steadfast and moved to her and kissed her hand, and while holding it firmly, looked into her eyes. She looked markedly sorry and impressed. "Can I give you head? Please!" I said beggingly.

Manuela moved with a startle and straightened her body position in the armchair. I could see her embarrassed eyes and could hear her panting. "Why do you want to give me head? I don't want it. I can't let you go down on me while we still have no relationship," she said with a slightly shivering voice and alternate breaks to gasp for air.

I thought I had reached my first goal. She was emotionally excited and hesitant about what to do next. I didn't give up. I said, "I promise nothing else will happen. I will not have sex with you. I won't take off any of my clothes, I promise. Trust me, as a friend!"

Manuela smiled. She said, "I don't know, it's a very strange situation. So have you been planning this all along? Was this dinner only an excuse for this?"

"I am sorry if I have annoyed you, but I've been thinking of you for the whole last two months," I said.

She didn't reply, but only glanced at me with her kind, ocean blue eyes. I went for her feet and kissed both of them. She didn't react. I moved my hands towards her zipper and opened the button and unzipped it. I let her slip out of her dark blue jeans slowly and gently. And then her beautiful, pink panty with the picture of a cute kitten on it.

She was sweet and juicy, and natural and unshaved. I read once in school that in paradise, there are fruits so succulent and lush that eating one of them is more pleasant than the whole fruits of our planet altogether, that nothing on earth is as delicious and tasty as them. But I doubt it now. I don't believe that they could be more luscious than Manuela's pussy.

◊   ◊   ◊

As I was experiencing the most pleasant moments of my life and as she was moaning with her delicate voice and venting her emotions with phrases in Spanish which I couldn't understand, the singer Chris Brown was singing my favorite song over the speakers in the background:

"…It's alright,

I'm not dangerous

When you're mine,

I'll be generous

You're irreplaceable, a collectible

Just like fine china…"

Made in the USA
Monee, IL
23 June 2024

60383554R00036